This is the fifth in the series of  :s.

Rainbow Twist uses their mindful power of kindness.

Mindfulness is a technique you can learn which involves noticing what's happening in the present moment, without judgement. You might take notice and be aware of your mind, body, and surroundings.

Mindfulness aims to help you:

- Become more self-aware.
- Feel calmer and less stressed.
- Feel more able to choose how to respond to your thoughts and feelings.
- Cope with difficult or unhelpful thoughts.
- Be kinder towards yourself.

I hope you enjoy getting to know each character as you join them on their adventures.

Love Sarah xx

www.justbemindfulness.com

The wind and the rain have turned Mind Island very grey and dull over the last few days. The Positivity Pets have been finding things to do inside as being outside isn't very enjoyable.

The Negative Nasties however, have been very active and loving the miserable weather. They thrive in this environment and know that the Positivity Pets often get gloomy on these grey days.

The Negative Nasties have been hanging around the Mindful Meadow and feeding from any negative thoughts that came from the Positivity Pets. They have enjoyed the grey skies and the constant rain.

A thunderstorm is heading towards Mind Island and the Negative Nasties are the only ones out and about this morning.

There had been thunderstorms for most of the day so Rainbow decided to invite a few friends round to play some board games.

Rainbow set out some drinks and snacks, lit the fire and got out the board games. Another rain cloud was heading towards Rainbow's house just as there was a knock on the door.

Sunshine was first to arrive and she brought some cakes.

Unicorn was next and she brought some homemade lemonade.

Ocean then arrived with a basket of fresh fruit for everyone to share.

They heard a rumble of thunder in the distance as the rain started to fall again. Rainbow welcomed them into the warmth and out of the cold.

The rain came down and bounced off the window sills of Rainbow's house. The Positivity Pets stood round the fire and dried off with a warm cup of tea.

"What a miserable day." said Unicorn to the group.

The Negative Nasties were drawn to Rainbow's house whilst the Positivity Pets were talking about how horrible the weather was. They peered through the kitchen window hoping to feed off any negativity coming from the Positivity Pets.

"We have a couple of visitors." said Rainbow looking out of the window.

" We can soon get rid of those Negative Nasties." replied Unicorn.

"I am so grateful for this rainy day as it has brought us together to play our favorite games." said Ocean.

The Positivity Pets focused on positive thoughts and combined their mindful powers of Kindness, Gratitude, Love and Happiness which soon scared the Negative Nasties away.

Rainbow topped up everyone's glasses with Unicorn's homemade lemonade whilst it was Ocean's turn to roll the dice.

The Positivity Pets soon forgot about the weather outside as they enjoyed each others company, board games, food and drinks.

The following morning, Rainbow was woken by beautiful sunshine coming through the bedroom curtains.

The birds were singing in the nearby trees as Rainbow drew the curtains and opened the window. There was a gentle breeze that carried the sweet smells of Spring.

"What a beautiful morning." thought Rainbow.

Rainbow enjoyed some dippy eggs and soilders for breakfast with a glass of fresh orange juice.

The morning sunshine came through the kitchen window, lighting up the room with a warm yellow glow.

Rainbow decided to take a walk through the Mindful Meadow and enjoy this beautiful day. As Rainbow took some slow breaths in of the morning air, Sunshine was up ahead looking a little sad.

"Good morning Sunshine, are you ok?" asked Rainbow.

"I'm not sure, I woke up feeling a bit down in the dumps." replied Sunshine.

"That's ok to feel like that. How about we take a walk together in the sunshine?" suggested Rainbow.

"I was just admiring the rainbow against the bright blue sky and how it is a reminder that the greater the storm, the brighter the rainbow." continued Rainbow.

Sunshine agreed to join Rainbow on a walk around Mind Island and together they noticed the Daffoldils and Tulips had started to bloom.

They walked up the hill and past Candy's house who they could hear singing to the radio in the background. This made Sunshine smile as she pictured Candy busy baking in her kitchen.

The birds were busy building a nest in the nearby tree and they too were singing to each other.

Rainbow and Sunshine decided to take a little break at the duck pond.

"Spring really is here." commented Sunshine as she sat on the tree stump next to the pond.

"The ducklings seem to be enjoying this nice weather, although they do love the rain too." replied Rainbow.

Sunshine's smile grew bigger as she watched the ducklings play together.

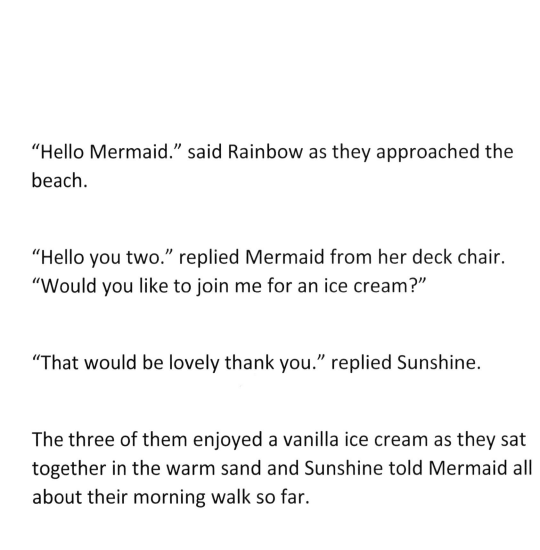

"Hello Mermaid." said Rainbow as they approached the beach.

"Hello you two." replied Mermaid from her deck chair. "Would you like to join me for an ice cream?"

"That would be lovely thank you." replied Sunshine.

The three of them enjoyed a vanilla ice cream as they sat together in the warm sand and Sunshine told Mermaid all about their morning walk so far.

Camo was busy clearing broken branches from last nights storm when Rainbow and Sunshine approached Camo Camp.

"Hello Camo, has there been much damage from the storm?" asked Rainbow.

"A little, however I can put all this broken wood to good use around the camp and the birds are finding the small twigs so useful for their nests." replied Camo.

"I guess there are always positives to be found." added Sunshine as she helped pick up some fallen branches.

"You have shown true kindness today Rainbow which I am so grateful for. Please let me make you some lunch to thank you for helping me feel happiness again." offered Sunshine.

Rainbow accepted Sunshine's kind invitation and they headed back through the Mindful Meadow towards Sunshine's house.

They enjoyed the warm sunshine on their faces and the smells of the wild flowers that surrounded them.

Sunshine welcomed Rainbow into her toadstool house and made them both a sandwich and a cup of tea.

They chatted about things they saw on their walk and how a little warm sunshine can make you feel so much brighter.

"Today has made me realise that feelings are not perminent and being sad will pass and can be replaced with happiness."

"Just like a rainbow after a storm." replied Rainbow with a smile.

Rainbow's mindful power of Kindness felt really strong after helping Sunshine feel happy again.

The Negative Nasties were nowhere to be seen and Rainbow smiled as a small rain cloud started to move across Mind Island.

This was a reminder that thoughts and feelings do pass and showing kindness to yourself and others can help when the negative thoughts and feelings show up.

That night, Rainbow took a glass of milk and a book to bed.

The sky was clear and bright with the stars twinkling in the light of the moon.

Rainbow drifted off to sleep feeling grateful for the day and for having the mindful power of Kindness to share with others.

The End.

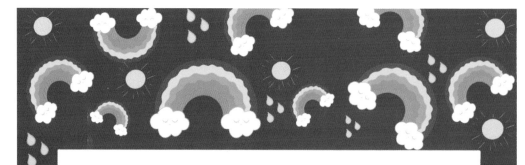

Have a chat about...

Rainbows mindful power is kindness. Has someone been kind to you today?

How did Rainbow show kindness to Sunshine?

Mindful breathing

www.justbemindfulness.com

Collect us all!

Positivity Pets

Characters available as pocket hugs, pocket pals and plushies. Options to add matching sensory stone and mindful breathing shapes.

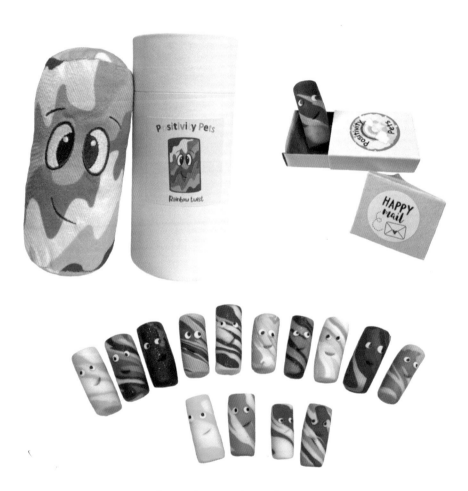

Printed in Great Britain
by Amazon

46336575R00025